ZOE'S ROOM
(No Sisters Allowed)

By Bethanie Deeney Murguia

ARTHUR A. LEVINE BOOKS
An Imprint of Scholastic Inc.

Zoe loves her room, especially at bedtime.

Every night, after Mama reads her one book, gives her one kiss, and turns out the light . . .

Zoe turns it right back on.
There is so much to be done.

She builds empires.

She explores uncharted territory.

She sets the table for morning tea with the royal court.

Then she gazes upon the stars.

But today, Mama has big news.
"Zoe, it's time for Addie to move out
of Mama and Papa's room.
She's going to be your roommate!"

"Hmph," says the queen.
"I believe *Dexter* has better manners."

Papa must not be listening.

"Not there!" screams Zoe. "That's the royal table."

But even the queen can't change this.

After one book, a kiss for Zoe, and a kiss for
her new roommate, Mama turns out the light.
"Now remember to be quiet so your sister can sleep."

Zoe is oh-so-quiet as she tiptoes across the room.

Click

"But I didn't make any noise," says Zoe.

The next night, the queen builds her empire.
"Shhh," she reminds the blocks.

The blocks do not behave.

On the fourth night, Zoe peers out her window. Where are the stars?

BOOM BOOM BOOM BOOM FLASH!

Thunder rumbles. Lightning flares.

The queen leaps for cover.

Addie stirs. She whimpers.
Then she snuggles close to Zoe.

Shhhooo—shhhooo—shhhooo.
Addie's breathing sounds like the ocean.

The queen drifts off to sleep,
dreaming of new worlds and new friends.

The next morning, Zoe sets another spot at her new table.
"Welcome, little queen," she says.
"Now drink your tea. There is so much to be done."

For my mom, who taught me to love books

Text and art copyright © 2013 by Bethanie Deeney Murguia

All rights reserved. Published by Arthur A. Levine Books, an imprint of Scholastic Inc., *Publishers since 1920.*
SCHOLASTIC and the LANTERN LOGO are trademarks and/or registered trademarks of Scholastic Inc.

Library of Congress Cataloging-in-Publication Data
Murguia, Bethanie Deeney.
Zoe's room (no sisters allowed) / by Bethanie Deeney Murguia. — 1st ed.   p. cm.
Summary: "Queen" Zoe protests having her sister Addie move from their parents' room
into her realm, but on the fourth night she has reason to be glad for a roommate.
ISBN 978-0-545-45781-1 (hardcover : alk. paper) [1. Sisters—Fiction.] I. Title.
PZ7.M944Zos 2013   [E]—dc2   2012016796

ISBN 978-0-545-45781-1

10 9 8 7 6 5 4 3 2 1   13 14 15 16 17

Printed in China   38   ·   First edition, June 2013

This book was made possible, in part, by a grant from the Society of Children's Book Writers and Illustrators.
The artwork was created in pen-and-ink and watercolor.
Book design by Chelsea C. Donaldson